Eveline F. Burt

Autumn Leaves

poems

Eveline F. Burt

Autumn Leaves
poems

ISBN/EAN: 9783337370787

Printed in Europe, USA, Canada, Australia, Japan

Cover: Foto ©Andreas Hilbeck / pixelio.de

More available books at **www.hansebooks.com**

Autumn Leaves.

Poems Written by

EVELINE F. BURT,

MT. GILEAD, OHIO.

CONTENTS.

AUTUMN LEAVES.

PREFACE.

POEMS BY E. F. BURT.

Complete May First, 1890.

This little book to friends is given,
May it remind of friends in heaven,
With kindest eyes as you read o'er
Pass by mistakes,—you have before.
I write for widows, orphans too,
Who proved their loyalty so true,
Whose fathers sleep on southern plain,
Whose husbands cannot come again.
Perhaps a thought some joy may bring
Some comfort to the sorrowing;
Bring back "old times" and sad good-bye
With sacred song I bring them nigh.
To those who once my pupils were,
I leave these Poems to your care;
Reminding you of pleasures past,
Of pleasant hours too bright to last.
Dear friends, I give to all of you
A loving thought both kind and true.

—E. F. B.

AUTUMN LEAVES.

Autumn leaves of many colors,
 Living but a day;
Oh! how very beautiful
 Falling to decay.

Sunlight passing through them
 Show their colors gay,
When a little wind storm
 Bloweth them away.

If my thoughts like Autumn leaves,
 Falling still are found;
Falling leaves are valuable,
 Will enrich the ground.

All things the most beautiful,
 Liveth not so long;
Gather all the Autumn leaves,
 Weave them into song.

Let life be not just breathing,
Give good to others while you are receiving
Let every breath be blessing,
 Every word be love,
In all weakness ask thy
 Help from heaven above.

LISTENING AND LED.

Listening my fathers voice,
    Led by His hand,
Casting my care on Him,
    Bravely I stand;
Listening to hear his will,—
    Follow I on ;
I will be thankful still,—
    Happy my song.

Led on in sorrows way,
    Calmly I trust ;
In darkness as in day,
    God's ways are just ;
Listening with thankful heart,
    Mercies I find ;
Led by His providence,
    Tenderly kind.

Listening my fathers calls,
    Angels attend ;
Open they Heaven's gate,
    Homeward I trend ;
Listening to hear His voice,
    Calling me near ;
Then all my journeyings,
    Evermore clear.

ONLY A NAME.

Only a name there's much
    More to me,
Many dear faces before
    Me I see.
Husband and brother, and
    Cousin and friend,
Went from our homes,
    Our lives to defend;
Husband, Oh! where can
    Your equal be found.
Brother, with laurel thy head
    We would crown,
Oh, friends of our childhood,
    Bright, noble and true,
You fought, bled and died for
    The red, white and blue.
We never may lay our sweet
    Flowers when you sleep;
Like Mary we cannot go
    There to weep.
How precious and sacred their
    Memory how dear,
Now proudly we honor the
    Names we find here.
We will bring brightest flowers
    To this sacred spot,
For not for one moment
    Shall they be forgot.

REUNION OF THE 96th O. V. I.

Oh! welcome dear soldiers,
　How proudly you come;
The battle is over
　The victory is won.
How gladly we hail you;
　So noble, so free,
May the land of our fathers
　Your home ever be.

Yet with all of our greeting,
　Our tears freely fall,
For we know that your number
　Is not there at all;
We forget not the warrior
　Who so bravely died,
To see our beloved ones
　We now are denied.

Then in your reunions
　Forget not the brave;
Oh! let this torn flag
　Still over them wave;
May God ever bless you,
　Protect you and keep,
Remember the warrior
　Your comrades asleep.

MINE.

It was a soldier's grave,
  So far away;
An honored life he gave,
  Alone he lay.

A star looked down from heaven
  On that dear mound,
The wind came whistling by,
  No other sound.

The moonbeams gentle light,
  Made night as day;
·Then morning came at last,
  Chased night away.

A little cloud o'erhung,
  A rain drop fell,
A bird sat near and sung
  A sad farewell.

The star was company
  I could not keep;
The raindrop was the tear
  I could not weep.

The bird sang him my song,
  From northern clime;
For, oh! this little mound,
  This grave was *mine.*

LIFE.

Our life-like shadows swiftly fly,
  Just like a flower were born to die,
Life as a vision in the night,
  Which fadeth in the morning light.

The snow flake with its fairy form
  Comes in a moment, then is gone,
So pure and white it glideth by
  To touch the earth, whisper good-bye.

A song is heard, we hear no more,
  The singers songs on earth are o'er,
Dear hands once pressed in silent love,
  Beckon us now from heaven above.

The blue eyes of our little child
  Awaken with the undefiled;
Our friend goes out with hurried feet,
  To walk no more our busy street.

A mother, well at eventide,
  We learn before the morn has died,
We're little children now at home,
  The years make haste and we are grown.

A mother's hair is turning grey,
  Who was a child, but yesterday,
The little child with curly head
  Will come ere long with manly tread.

A bride is at the altar given,
  A year is gone, the tie is riven;
For life is but a summer day
  On all things written, pass away.

HYMN.

Jesus my Redeemer King,
  Of thy praises let me sing;
Let me put my hand in thine,
  Being led by hand divine,
I am weak, but thou art strong,
  Help me Lord to follow on.

I would hide beneath thy wing,
  Sheltered I can truly sing,
But my Savior knoweth best
  Whether I need pain or rest;
I am weak, but thou art strong,
  Help me Lord to follow on.

I would bring myself to thee
  Poor and helpless though I be;
Lay myself low at thy feet,
  Knowing thou wilt work complete,
I am weak, but thou art strong,
  Help me Lord to follow on.

There are things so hard to bear,
  Yet I know the Lord doth care,
Sometimes Lord there's much to take;
  Let me bear them for thy sake,
I am weak, but thou art strong,
  Help me Lord to follow on.

If I love my Saviour more,
  When these trials all are o'er;
If the shadows lead to light,
  Day will come after the night,
I am weak, but thou art strong,
  Help me Lord to follow on.

SCRIPTURE PEARLS.

———◆———

Ask and ye shall receive,
Believe and ye shall live,
Cast all your care upon the Lord,
    So willing to forgive.

Delight thyself upon the Lord,
Enter the narrow way,
Fear not, I'm with thee to the end,
    Will make thy night as day.

Give to the Lord the glory due,
Hide thou beneath the rock,
I am the life, the truth, the way,
    The shepherd of the flock.

Jesus our Savior Priest and King,
Knoweth the righteous way,
Loveth the young to trust in Him,
    Seeks those who go astray.

My sheep He calls them all by name,
Not one of them is lost,
Often the blind and halt are healed,
    To them there is no cost.

Pray without ceasing, He will hear,
Quench not the spirit's power,
Remember He will hear thy cry
    In every trying hour.

Sufficient to the day it is
The evil load to bear,
Unless the cross by Thee is borne,
    The crown you cannot wear.

Venture upon the Lord most high,
Why will you longer wait,
Examine well your hope of heaven,
    Before it is too late.

Ye must be born again to live,
Zealous and faithful grow,
And after all to Christ is given,
    Confess 'tis all I owe.

BOX OF OLD LETTERS.

Dear old letters laying here,
  They remind of old friends dear,
Crumbling in the dust with age
  Time has written on each page.

Here are letters not a few,
  This was written in thirty-two
Penned by my mother's hand,
  When a bride in a strange land.

Of privation it will tell,
  Loneliness and funeral knell,
Crumbling letter left to me,
  Treasured shall this letter be.

Time worn letters breathing still
  Of the love her heart did fill,
Precious letter, folded hand,
  Mother's in a better land.

Then another, older still,
  Speaks of Grandma ever will,
For affectionate and kind
  Dear old Grandmamma we find.

In the answer Grandpa speaks,
  My dear wife I'd like to meet,
Then he writes when God is near
  You and I will never fear.

Though you are so far away,
  From His care you cannot stray;
Crumble letter into dust,
  Live forever Grandpa must.

Here's another time has worn
  With age yellow, places torn,
This torn letter I revere,
  Grandma Great penned these words here.

Eighteen twelve, Great Grandma said,
  In God's ways I wish to tread,
Teach your children God to fear
  From an aged mother dear.

All these letters careful hold,
  Traced by hands all still and cold ;
These dear friends come not again,
  In our hearts they live the same.

Here are traced kind, loving words,
  Dear sweet voices never heard ;
For they come to us no more,
  Never as they did before.

Lay these letters safely by,
  They shall speak to you and I
When these friends we once more greet,
  May our number be complete.

THE OLD LOG HOUSE.

How well I remember the old log house,
  The home where I was born ;
And happy days that were spent therein,
  On my own dear father's farm.

CHORUS.

What a happy time we children had
  As the evening hours drew on,
We sang our songs, and played our games,
  Oh, happy days long gone.

Oh, there was light in the old back log,
  There was music in mother's song,
And the stories she'd tell before the fire
  In the days that have long since gone.
                              —[Chorus.

Those happy hours have passed away,
  Dear father and mother are gone,
And brothers and sisters are growing gray,
  Who lived on the old, old farm.
                              —[Chorus.

No other home in our later years,
  Since our old log house has gone,
Were ever as bright as in those days,
  Of childhood story and song.
                              —[Chorus.

EIGHTY-NINE.

O, year so fraught with sorrow
        Eighty-nine,
Through all thy days we trace
        A hand divine,
Death coming here and there
        With silent tread,
Numbering this one, and that one,
        With the dead.
The glad new year when,
        Richest gifts abound,
Slowly and silently without
        A sound.

The maiden fair, the little child
Went home to heaven with
        Garments undefiled;
The man who pitied others
        In distress,
Who only lived that others
        He might bless;
The husband whose strong arm
        Could shield
The wife so well beloved,
        Must to thee yield.
The loving daughter with her
        Power to charm,
Goes gladly where no accident
        Can harm.
Not for the widow or the orphans tears
        Would death delay
Its freezing touch, no love
        Or power could stay;
The man of fourscore years
        And three,
The mother with her babe
        So wee.
The maiden, who made glad
        Our hearts with song,
Who will be missed for years,
        In church, and choir, and throng,
The youngest of the flock torn
        From a mother's arms.

Emptied she said, but taken
　　From all harm.
The old man bent with age,
　　With eyes so dim,
Awakened not then he was
　　Gathered in;
For silvery hair, and childhood
　　With its love of truth
The one's in middle life, the—
　　Gay and sparkling youth,
Alike have fallen, since on
　　Christmas day
We sat and laughed our time away.

We meet no more these dear ones
　　On our busy street,
We may not wait a moment this
　　Dear aged friend to greet;
We look in vain, there's only *now*
　　An empty chair;
The one we loved and prized will
　　Never more be there.
Perhaps there is an empty shoe
　　We lay away;
A little curl, that on the dear
　　Head lay,
A penciled mark upon the Bible
　　Tells
The truth the one believed and
　　Where our loved one dwells.

AUTOGRAPH.

The past is not our own, '
　　The present moment flies;
The future to us is unknown,
　　May open to other eyes;
Now in this world we live—
　　To love and bless,
How then can we afford
　　To love each other less.

OLD TIMES.

Old times will linger ever near the heart;
Which later years so fraught with care,
Can never from us part
All that we loved in sunny childhood days,
When we found beneath the forest trees
Fine places for our plays.
'Twas before the mighty woodman
Laid the forest trees so low;
That we would gather acorns,
For our dishes make them do.
Then our pretty little carpet
Was a bright and mossy green;
We children had a good time,
Within our grape vine swing.
At that time the people lived
In their cabins built of logs;
With stick chimneys on the outside,
All were happy, what's the odds;
Other neighbors lived the same,
The country then was new,
We thought it not a hardship
To make a little do.
When we would have log rollings
We would ask our neighbors in,
Take the door down for a table,
You ought to there have been.
Our stove was just a fire place,

We hung the kettle on the crane;
And fried our meat upon the coals,
It tasted better all the same.
If friends came to spend the evening,
They put us all to bed;
We tried our best to keep awake
And hear all that was said.
We were taught then to remember,
To listen, softly tread;
To keep quite still as children should
Within our trundle bed.
Well, people did not attend church,
To show the latest style;

Their dress was woven home-spun,
At their bonnets you would smile,
Their garments now would look quite odd
Were then in fashion new,
Their fortune was not on their back,
They made a little do.
Dear loving friends of days gone by,
Kind faithful man of God;
Who led our church and Sabbath school
Are mouldering 'neath the sod.
Oh! dear old friends, Oh! childhood home,
Will not be ours again,
Yet when we sing a cheerful song;
An olden time refrain.
I see beloved faces
Around my father's door,
I almost hear the footsteps
Of those who come no more.

HEAVEN.

A home in Heaven! oh, how sweet,
Within that home joy is complete.
A home where all the weary Rest;
Sweet home where dwell the truly blest.

Oh, Heavenly home of quiet rest,
Our Father's house, and mansion blest.
We prize too much our home on earth,
Forget our home of priceless worth;
Our eyes shall turn anew to thee,
Where Jesus said the "mansions be,"
Prepared for those who love Him well,
Where holy, happy angels dwell.

Eye hath not seen, nor ear hath heard,—
The beauties of the lovely land,
Nor can the heart of man conceive
The music of the Heavenly band.

THE BIBLE.

Neglected book of priceless worth,
  The best of all to mortals given,
Thy truth the mind can ne'er bring forth,
  Yet find enough to guide to heaven.

All books complete borrowed from thee,
  All of real worth was thy bequest;
Oh! what would fallen man not be
  If by thy truth we were not blest.

In ages past e'er knowledge, art,
  Or any science had progressed,
The truth like magic on the heart
  Made the proud soul its sins confess.

And, oh, when sorrow 'round us throw,
  A gloom which earth can never light,
'Tis to thy pages we may go
  ·And find a home where all is bright.

Oh! precious, but neglected book,
  So dear to every Christian's heart;
I'll hold thee fast, let my *last look*
  Be to the Christ e'er I depart.

AUTOGRAPH.

Seek to be pure in heart,
To have thy thoughts refined,
Thy body is but crumbling dust;
Seek then to store the mind.
The little deeds show how we build,
Those lives 'with daily duty filled,
Can never live for naught.
Build high, true greatness shall be thine,
True wisdom not of earth divine;
In sinful ways may you not fall,
This is the way to measure tall.

THE OLD ARM CHAIR.

How dear to my heart is the old arm chair,
    That sat by the old fireside;
And the best of reasons I'll give to you,
    In that chair my mother died.

I see her now as she sat therein,
    In the days that have long gone by;
How little then we thought of it,
    In this chair our mother should die.

The old arm chair was a resting place,
    When the day of toil was o'er;
Tw as there she was carried by angel hands,
    Where she will be tired no more.

The old arm chair is vacant now,
    Nor will I ever again,
See the dear old face I loved so well,
    For mother is free from pain.

Dear friends, have you an old arm chair,
    A mother to fill it the same?
Thank God each morn as you kiss her lips,
    For she may not long remain.

AUTOGRAPH.

May friends not bought
With gold be thine;
May love and truth
Thy life refine;
Nor may a shadow,
Cloud thy brow.
Let loving thoughts,
Thy heart endow;
May gentle words,
And deeds complete,
Embalm thy life,
And make it sweet.
As daughter, sister,
Husband, friend,
The God of Heaven,
Thee, defend.

"WE WILL GO TO HER."

Dear child of our affection,
  Our Mamie, dear and true;
We wonder in selecting,
  Death should have chosen you.

For in night's solemn stillness,
  An angel band unseen,
Took thee from those who loved thee,
  Mid anguish, lasting keen.

Dear loving hands are clasping,
  Dear tender heart so true;
With all our tears and fasting,
  We grieve, but not for you.

Your rosy lips caressing,
  Once lisped in love our name;
Your busy feet are resting,
  Not tossed in weary pain.

Dark loving eyes unfolding,
  To glories never seen;
Your Saviour now beholding
  By living pastures green.

Like Israel's sweet Psalmist,
  We know you cannot come;
We hope to find our Mamie
  When all our work is done.

The flowers you wished to gather
  To place on mother's grave,
We place with sweet mementoes,
  With those your school-mates gave.

And there are flowers immortal,
  And songs of highest worth,
And Mamie's voice is being tuned
  To songs ne'er heard on earth.

ALONE.

Alone, did you say, dear friend?
With God and the angels near.
Can't you hear His voice
Bid your heart rejoice,
Take my hand dear child, I'm here.

Alone, did you say, dear friend?
Why, the widow's God is thine;
You are fed each day
In Elijah's way
By a hand that is divine.

Alone, did you say, dear friend?
Was it ever told how far
Is the golden gate for which you wait,
The home where your loved ones are?

Alone, did you say, dear friend?
Wait only a little while;
It won't be long,
With the ransomed throng,
Your song with theirs unite.

Alone, did you say dear friend?
It won't seem long that day,
At the golden gate,
Where loved ones wait
To meet you on the way.

LITTLE ALLIE.

Darling little Allie,
With her eyes of blue,
Loving, wise and true;
Same old story told,
She will not grow old,
    Darling little Allie.

Grandma's little Allie,
Trotting here and there,
Found most anywhere;
With her loving smile,
Helping all the while,
    Once was little Allie.

Grandpa's little Allie,
Climbing on his knee,
Loving there to be.
Resting tired feet,
Then she falls asleep,
    Tired my little Allie.

Mother's little Allie,
Was so tired that day,
When she went away.
Allie's busy feet
Walk the golden street,
    In Heaven is little Allie.

Darling little Allie,
Is a jewel, rare,
In the angels care.
For our Allie waits
By the golden gate,
    Darling little Allie.

BE STILL.

Be still, oh, loving heart, be still,
Oh, hear thy Master's voice and will;
He took thy young wife home,
He took her from her husband's side,
That you might more in Him confide;
Yield to your Maker's will.

CHORUS.

Be still, oh, loving heart, be still,
He'll keep her from all earthly ill,
And shield her from all earthly harm.

Be still, oh, loving heart, be still,
Oh, wait thy Father's voice and will;
He took thy husband home,
You think him sleeping in his grave,
He lives who died your soul to save,
Does thy desires fulfill.

—[Chorus.

Be still, oh, loving heart be still,
He'll keep thy little child, He will ;
He took thy sweet babe home,
That he might shield it from all harm ;
Sure, you would follow safely on
Where your dear child had gone.

—[Chorus.

THE SINGER AND THE SONG.

DELLA BARTON.

I think of the singer,
Who gladdened our hearts,
And made it re-echo with song;
I think of the song,
As she warbled it forth
In such strains—
As to angels belong,

I think of the singer—
As singing on,
Just over the river side;
I think of the song—
As being sung,
For its re-echo
Never has died.

I think in the choir—
With the angels above,
We'll find both singer and song;
For the music the singer—
Made while here
Would gladden an
Angel throng.

Oh, singer sweet of—
An angels throng,
Oh, come to us once again;
Oh, beautiful song,
Awaken our hearts,
In welcome and
Sweet refrain.

Oh, choir where the
Singer never shall tire!
Oh, singer, in robes made white.
Oh, song of immortal,—
Glory and bliss,
Sing on in your
Sweet delight.

FAREWELL.

I leave my husband's grave,
  So far away;
My heart shall linger here,
  I cannot stay.

Oh, let me kiss the sod,
  O'er his dear clay.
Let me stand closely by,
  While yet I may,

Oh, star of gentle night,
  Look down from the sky.
Stand guard o'er this dear mound.
  When I'm not by.

And moonbeam's gentle light
  Make night as day.
Oh leave him not alone
  When I'm away.

Sweet bird, oh! sing with me
  My sad farewell ,
And rain-drop mingle tears
  That oft have fell.

Oh, let me sweetly sleep
  When life is past;
By my own husband's side,
  Sweet rest at last,

LINES TO A BROTHER DEAD.

Death came once more, with relentless tread,
And numbered a dear one with the dead;
They folded his hands on his manly breast,
And closed his eyes as is wont to rest.
'Twas the mouldering clay of one we loved,
The soul from its casket had been removed.
We could not watch it in its upward flight,
Just the form was left for our mortal sight.
Then the mourners came, and the house was
     dark,
And each heart was sad, then the tear would
     start;
And the watchers waited, with calm, still tread,
While the coffin plated for its narrow bed.
The morning came with its bright sunlight;
The birds were warbling with pure delight.
All nature seemed in its gayest dress,
While cold lips waited their last caress.
Then many came with mournful look,
While the pastor read from the dear old book.
"If a man die—shall he live again?"
Doth Jesus care for our mortal frame,
Though dust shall return to the dust again—
The power of Christ shall remain the same.
Then words of comfort to the mourner spoke:
That Jesus would help them bear the stroke,
The mourners gazed on the dear, cold dead,
For the prayer was offered and the bible read;
Yet God could comfort—the mourner bless;
'Twas he who had made their number less.

'Twas **a** mournful scene, when the parting
     came,
For a darling son in the grave was lain ;
Then they laid the dust on the coffin deep,
Then hoped again in Heaven to meet.

In Heaven there is no sad farewell,
There those who love Jesus forever shall
     dwell,
Remember dear mourner, to lean on Him still
And list to His voice, and follow His will.

VELMA.

"I was dumb, I opened not my mouth because
Thou didst it."

There's a dear little girl who is missing to·
night,
Yet we claimed her a few days ago;
No doubt she is singing with angels so bright,
Though her dear precious form lies so low.

There's a place in our hearts none but Velma
can fill,
Little clothes that we can bear to see;
A young loving heart that is silent and still,
Oh! we wonder sometimes can it be?

There's a sweet little voice that could sing,
oh, so sweet,
Which has sung its last warble below;
We have but to wait dear Velma to meet
Where such beautiful flowers will grow.

Those flowers the brightest fade first from our
sight,
And God often chooses our fireside to blight,
Yet we know when clouds darken a fair April
sky,
That there will be sunshine to cheer us by
and by.

LOLA.

A little bud was taken,
By the Saviour's hand ;
That it might open
In a better land.
It shall not be blighted
By the frosts of time;
Our darling shall be cared for
By a hand divine.

MY FATHER'S OLD FARM.

How close to my life are the
  Memories of childhood,
And fond recollections bring back to
  My view;
The maple and oak in the
  Far spreading wildwood,
Those days when fond hearts were
  Most loving and true.

The wide-spreading oak, with the
  Maple tree by it,
The green grassy knoll, and the
  Nice shady dell;
The dear old farm house,
  With the road running by it,
In sight of the school and
  The clear sounding bell.

The nice shady walk where we
  Children would wander,
The orchard and meadow,
  And grain-laden field;
Those places for us were
  An infinite pleasure,
No other such treasure
  Can ever more yield.

Our father once viewed it
  With eyes overflowing,
On home, its attractions
  Would lovingly dwell;
On fruits of the year hardest
  Labor bestowing,
Our father's dear farm
  Where we so loved to dwell.

Now lonely it seems as we
  Children pass by it,
The orchard, and meadow,
  And grain-laden field;

With longing we look, oft wish
   We could buy it,
This home of our birth-place,
   Such pleasure could yield.

Dear father and mother,
   Are quietly sleeping,
Awaken no more
   To welcome us there;
Let us meet them above
   With a happier greeting,
And share evermore
   In an infinite love.

INCIDENT.

One day I called on an aged pair,
The time seemed long since I'd been there;
And age had frosted the good man's hair
Who sat by his wife in his easy chair.
While her form was bent, all the love was
   there
For the good old man, with the frosted hair;
Four score years, and almost ten,
Like birds in a nest they had always been;
A day at a time had lived and then
Would both go *home* in the morning.
This dear old wife of great renown,
Had *Cooked* for the men who laid out our town,
And said on the place she had tried to frown,
With its towering hills to be cut down.
The hills shall 'round old Gilead stand,
When they shall look on the better land
With others who lived in dear old G——,
Who have toiled so hard for you and me.

MULTIPLIED.

Elisha heard the voice of God,
Went on the way Elijah trod;
For boldly would the Prophet tell
The faults of Kings, and do it well.
A woman lived within the land,
Whose husband 'mong the Prophets stand;
When good Elisha passed that way,
She called to him without delay;
And said thy servant feared the Lord,
I know thou wilt not doubt my word.
The creditors approach I dread,
Since he, my husband is now dead.
My two dear sons still left to me,
As bondsmen will now taken be.
Elisha said, O, pray tell me
What would'st thou have me do for thee?
Thy handmaid has one pot of oil
With which the creditors to foil.
He said, go borrow vessels more,
And bring them emptied to thy door—
Of all thy neighbors, not a few,
Then shut thy door thy sons and you.
Then fill the empty vessels fast,
'Till you have filled the very last;
As fast as filled, oh, set aside
While you within the room abide.
Then she went in, shut too the door,
The boys brought vessels, she would pour;
When she had filled and not delayed,
Behold the oil, for it had stayed.
With joy she did the good news tell,
Elisha said this oil you sell;
This my poor woman, my request,
Go pay thy debt, live on the rest.
The widow, God will not forsake,
Nor thy two sons as bondsmen take.
Oh! learn a lesson widowed friend,
Always on God the Lord depend;
He can increase thy little store,
When not enough can make it more;
Then trust Him for thy daily bread,.
Be it enough the Lord hath said.

ANGELS.

I want to be an angel,
　And by the needy stand ;
With a bushel of potatoes
　"And flour sack in my hand."
I'd love to wipe the tear drops
　From the lonely care-worn face,
As much as lieth in me,
　The lost one to replace.

I'd love to be an angel,
　On earth to take a stand;
For all that's noble, good and true,
　In our all glorious land.
Against all wrong too great and small,
　I'd live for God and right ;
The truly good should be the tall,
　The great in God's own sight.

No one can be an angel,
　In spotless robes made white,
For angels we must wait awhile,
　'Till there shall be no night.
But we may do an angel's work
　In ministering to the poor,
For only they who try it once
　Can know what they endure.

Oh ! would you like an angel,
　One day with angels stand,
Give to the poor and needy,
　Nor with a sparing hand.
Let tender tear drops moisten,
　While others grief you share ;
Don't stop with just a bushel,
　Give all that you can spare.

BLOSSOMS.

In the golden summer
  When all earth was bright,
All for us was darkened
  In our home, 'twas night.

Little hands were folded,
  Still our baby's tread,
In her little casket
  Lay our Annie *dead*.

Little face so lovely,
  Prattling lips so still,
Oh, we miss our darling
  Now and ever will.

Just like a fair lily
  Broken from the stem,
Yet our dear one liveth
  In God's diadem.

Little Annie liveth
  In the Shepherd's fold,
When the morning cometh
  Shareth joys untold.

————o————

In snowy robes of spotless white,
  In little coffin lay;
The idle of our heart and home,
  Our darling little May.

Those eyes which shone with
  Heaven's own light,
And clustering golden hair;
  Dear little hands and busy feet,
Need not a mother's care.

The night of death came all too soon,
  And clouded o'er the day;
The tender Shepherd took our lamb
  And carried her far away.

J. S. H.

—o—

Oh, how we miss him,
 Aching hearts await;
Until we shall meet him
 At the golden gate.

Oh, how we miss him—
 Miss him everywhere;
We can almost see him
 Going here and there.

Oh, *we shall miss him,*—
 Truly are bereft,
Youngest and last one,
 Sweet be thy rest.

Others will not miss him,
 Loving hearts await ;
Dear ones were waiting
 At the golden gate.

MOTHER'S CHOIR.

The singers were many, the song was free,
The place to sing was an apple tree.
Then it was a song you could have all free,
No matter how poor in pocket you be,
If you'd only get up in the morning.
The singer sang in the early spring,
In the morning bright would gladness bring.
With a hop and a skip on busy wings,
Would find a bug, or a little string ;
Would build their nest in the morning.
Oh, robin, sweet with your gladsome song,
We will learn a lesson as we go along ;
If we would be wise or wealthy or strong.
We must get up in the morning.

THE TEMPERANCE ARMY.

There's a war cloud of temperance revived,
   There are workers for Christ coming on ;
Yes the time for grand work has arrived,
   Will you tell to which side you belong?
There are banners afloat in the sky,
   There are those to be snatched from the
      grave ;
When sin and destruction is nigh
   There is One who is mighty to save.

You have heard of the snares they have laid,
   You have heard of the dreadful saloon ;
You have heard how the mighty and brave
   Are snatched from the jaws of the tomb.
Have you heard of the brave and the true
   Who are coming by ten thousand strong ?
O, say, my young friend, is it you
   Who will to this army belong ?

Then away with this curse from our land,
   There's a grand jubilee drawing nigh ;
Young man, let them know where you stand,
   To darkness and sin say good bye ;
There's a place for your name on the scroll,
   There's a work that your Master has given ;
There's a ransom once paid for your soul,
   There are loved ones awaiting in heaven.

JOHNNY.

I was going home from a visit,
   Had kissed my kind friend adieu ;
When with arms outstretched, little Johnny
   Said, " pease, me too."

How we loved the dear little fellow,
   Nor thought soon his absence to weep ;
Yet, with all of our loving, the Saviour
   Took dear little Johnny to keep.

PROFILE.

His form was bent, his hair was gray,
His eye could see most every way,
His voice would sound like a distant roar,
When a tardy scholar came in the door;
The ruler and rod were the fashion then,
No one would have liked to have tardy been.

We sang our Geography lessons o'er,
Like the printed chart studied before;
We swept the school house at noon for pay
While the lazy ones were out at play,
Then when the master at noon came in
We were the ones his favor to win.

Gold dollars were given for prizes new
To those who were the industrious few,
A new school book would he thrown in
For those who would try his favor to win;
So thorough in work, so earnest and brave,
We will not forget the lessons he gave.

No one ever taught in our dear old town,
Who earned for himself a greater renown,
And while we remember the school days of old,
His memory to us is as good as his gold;
There are those in the east, there are those in
    the west,
There are those who have long since gone to
    rest,
Who owe to this teacher their success here,
Will always the name of this teacher revere.

We shall not forget those dear old school days,
The old round school house, our master's
    stern ways;
This school house once stood southeast of the
    square,
Our fondest remembrance shall ever be there.

ASLEEP.

Sleep, dear mother, sweetly sleep,
While o'er thy couch thy children weep;
    We loved thee, Jesus loved thee more,
And welcomed thee to heaven's shore.

Sleep, mother, as we look upon thy face,
We know no other one can fill thy place;
    No other step so welcome at our door,
Thy busy fingers doeth kind deeds never more.

Sleep, mother sleep, we may not hear thy
        voice,
Nor share with thee our pleasant New Year's
        joys,
    But notes of praise in heaven are tuned anew,
And beauties rare presented to thy view.

Sleep, darling mother, calmly sleep,
While loving memories we, thy children keep;
    Of all thy loving care, instruction kind,
And blest example left to those behind.

Sleep, mother, sleep, thou wilt awake again,
To life anew, and joys without a pain;
    We will not think of thee, as sleeping 'neath
        the sod,
But with the Angels, thy loved ones and God.

Sleep, mother, thy last, long, silent sleep,
Within the lonely tomb to us so deep;
    Jesus has called thee, waiting at the door,
Our mother liveth and has only gone before.

FASHION'S QUESTION BOX.

Will you tell me how my new dress should be
    made?
Can you show me how these folds are to be laid?
Should I wear brown, black or the navy blue?
Do you think the folds of my dress are true?
Do you think they'd know if this goods were
        pieced?
Will the trimming hide where it is creased?
Should I wear a hat that is quite tall?
Say, ain't this hat for me too small?
Is her hat trimmed in the latest style?
Don't a pretty hat your heart beguile?
Does a turban hat look good on me?
Oh, ain't that hat as lovely as it can be?
Which suits me best, a bonnet or a hat?
Don't you wish you could wear a feather like
        that?
Will the bonnet be quite large or small?
Will the crown of the hat be low or tall?
I have not been to church for a great long
        while,
Because my clothes are out of style.
Oh, dear, that girl is far too small,
I think she is laced to death, that's all?
I know dear mother must work all night,
But we girl's hands must be so white.
The old folks now must keep out of the way,
For the dear young people must have their say.
These questions and thoughts are for common
        clay,
Shall we hope dear friends for a better day?

REST AWHILE.

Come, come my heart, Oh! take a little rest,
　What would'st thou now, oh what is thy re-
　　quest?
These cravings will not bring Thee thy desire
　Except thou cease thy longings, *look up
　　higher.*

Would'st thou have wealth to lay it at His feet?
　Lay down thy will, 'tis to thy Lord more
　　sweet,
For he who has but little may give more,
　To give at all must sacrifices make o'er and
　　o'er.

Woud'st thou have honor, spread thy fame
　　abroad,
　Think more of self, than thou dost think
　　of God?
He who hath made thee can in a moment take
　Thy gifts, if thou dost Him forsake.

Or if thou would'st have love to help Thee
　　bear thy part,
　And love not thy maker with all thy heart,
All love like this will surely leave a smart,
　And all thy joys shall quickly from thy life
　　depart

Oh, cease thy craving, rest a little while,
　There is no love without a tear, in truest
　　hearts some guile;
Contented would'st thou be, rest in thy lot,
　Take things as they are, thou shall not be
　　forgot.

There's *one* who knows Thee will not mis
　　construe,
　Nor take thee wrong whatever thou shalt do,
One lasting friend thou can'st always secure;
　He is a friend who evermore endures,
Thy wants may all be met, if thou in Christ
　　abide,
　In all thy sorrows in the Rock of Ages hide.

HIDDEN.

A worm came crawling that had sixteen feet,
A worm with thirteen joints complete;
When all at once so still it lay,
You would think the ugly thing meant to stay.
It was only undoing its clothes behind,
A newer dress underneath to find;
The dress it had on was far too small,
That was the reasons it could not crawl.
Four times it leaves a dress behind,
Always a clean new one to find;
The last time it tries it is stiff and cold,
You would think as you watch its sorrows
    were told,
That the ugly worm would trouble no more
Creeping and crawling around your door,
When you are delighted to see one day
A golden-tipped butterfly sailing away,
On beautiful wings in the bright sunlight,
A thing of beauty and pure delight.
How like this worm do we travel along,
Never seeming to know to what state we
    belong;
There are many old garments that we should
    lay by
Before our pure spirits soar aloft to the sky.

HOODS.

Childhood is the morning,
    'Tis the spring-time hour,
And the precious seed time
    Gather we the flower.

Then comes fairy girlhood,
    Boyhood needing care,
Maidenhood and manhood
    With their do and dare.

Womanhood and motherhood,
    Love and joy shall cling,
Every good there is in life
    With these hoods we bring.

Motherhood is full of song,
    With its gifts so rare,
Widowhood means struggle on
    With the Lord to care.

ADA.

It was a wintry day, yet rain drops sped,
  And wept sweet tears for the early dead;
As if to moisten the hard, cold earth,
  To grieve with us as they bore her forth.

The gentle rain drops seemed to say,
  No bitter tears should be shed to-day;
Why grieve for those in that happy home,
  Where none are sick, weary or lone?

Let this darling child sleep on and rest,
  Fold our sisters hands upon her breast;
Speak softly she will not hear you now,
  Kiss for the last our dear one's brow.

Call, she will answer you never more,
  She waiteth upon a far off shore;
We will for the last with flowers adorn,
  Then look for the last on the lovely form.

We will listen, the kind words our pastor
    shall say,
  Then prayerfully, tearfully, bear her away;
To lay her to rest in the silent tomb,
  From which our dear Saviour has taken
    the gloom.

Dear friends, will you think of the streets of
    pure gold,
  Where eye hath not seen, neither tongue
    has it told;
Think of the pleasures with those who are
    there,
  Of the fadeless robes that the holy wear.

Hands clasped in hands, no more to be
    severed,
  Homes broken here, shall there be re-
    gathered;
Think, would you bring back to sorrow and
    pain
  The sister and daughter to see once again?

One of our teachers, a friend so esteemed,
  Has only gone home, is with the redeemed,
Entwined in the hearts of beloved ones is
    she,
  Treasured forever dear Ada shall be.

Now father, and brother, and sisters are
    there,
  The robes and the crown of the holy they
    wear,
How sweetly and fondly will welcome be given
  To us by beloved ones rejoicing in heaven.

CHATTANOOGA.

———◆———

Beautiful burial place of our dead,
With the white marble at each soldier's head,
Beautiful place, by a nation revered,
Sacred thy pathways to true hearts endeared,
Our brave men who died that we might be free,
Are sleeping their last in old Tennessee.
I see the dear face of my brother so fair
Whose eyes were as blue as the sky shineth
    there,
Whose heart was as true as this earth ever knew
There this brother sleepeth 'neath the red,
    white and blue.
A sister's dear husband is resting near by,
So strong and so manly, so noble to die,
Oh, would I could go there and sit close beside
The graves of these martyrs our joy and our
    pride,
Across the great waters on fair southern plain,
Our husband, our brothers shall not come again,
The rain-drop shall moisten, the star looketh
    down,
The sweet bird is singing its song of renown.
All nature shall smile o'er the place of our dead
The place we so fondly could wish we might
    tread,
Oh ! think of our dead in old Tennessee,
Who died that your life might be noble and free.

———◆———

W. R. C. AND G. A. R.

———◆———

W. R. C. and G. A. R.
Join these letters with a star,
Spread your kind deeds far and wide ;
Let no rivalry divide.
Long as stars shall light the sky,
Work there is for you and I,
Woman, let your works abound,
Works of love to all around.
With relief in time of need
Corps of ready workers speed ;
G. A. R. and W. R. C.
Work for God and liberty.

Grand and noble, loyal brave,
Army hurrying to the grave,
Well may this Republic show
Honor to the brave and true,
While the stars and stripes shall wave,
Honor we our soldier's brave ;
G. A. R. and W. R. C.
Work for God and liberty.

HIDDEN PRAYER.

———o———

Our Father over all the earth,
Who art the ruler of the universe,
In heaven, on earth, we will exclaim
Hallowed be Thy holy name.
Thy Kingdom over all shall be,
Come, worship then this King with me,
Thy tribute to the King of Kings
Will be a loyal heart to bring.
Done, is the willing service done?
On earth the path of life begun;
As it is finished *in* the sky,
Heaven, shall the covenant ratify.
Give us, Oh, Lord, the grace to see,
This day we should remember Thee,
Our daily bread, wilt thou supply—
And feed us ere we faint and die.
Forgive us for we sinful art
All of *our tresspasses* in heart,
As we our foes in truth forgive,
Forgive our sins, and let us live,
Those whom we willingly forgive,
Who trespass 'gainst us, oh, receive.
Lead us not in temptation's way,
But deliver us from evil day,
For thine is the Kingdom, and the power,
And the glory forever more.

SERVICE.

———o———

As God is my Creator kind,
For me my life in him I find,
And give my talents, power and all,
My life surrender to his call.
House, money, land, to us is given,
We use them for ourselves and heaven,
Will lay them at our master's feet;
Serve him in voice and song complete,
The willing service, we will give,
Lord, us accept, and bid us live.